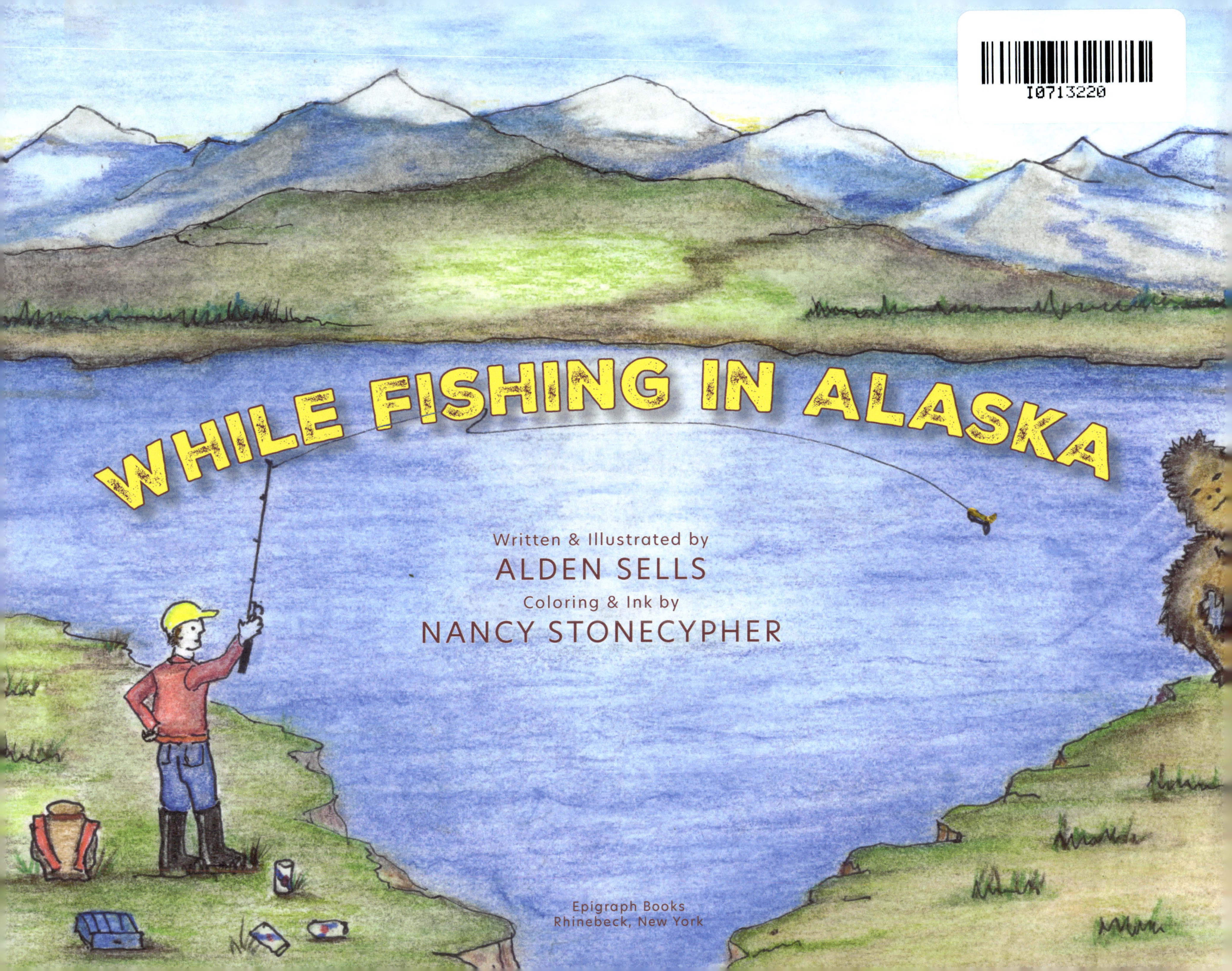

WHILE FISHING IN ALASKA
Written & Illustrated by
ALDEN SELLS
Coloring & Ink by
NANCY STONECYPHER
Epigraph Books
Rhinebeck, New York

Other Books by Alden Sells

Do All Dogs Go to Heaven When They Die?
My Friend Was Trying to Tell Me
If They Don't Let Dogs in Heaven

ISBN 978-1-960090-15-7

Written by Alden Sells
Illustrations by Alden Sells
Coloring and ink by Nancy Stonecypher
Layout by Colin Rolfe
Proofing and Editing by Robin Sells

Epigraph Books
22 East Market Street, Suite 304
Rhinebeck, NY 12572
(845) 876-4861
epigraphps.com

For the Cordova Cowboy Crew (you know who you are),
and more specifically Steve J - the closest thing
to a Sasquatch that I've ever had the pleasure to
mix it up with!

Keep Squatchin' My Friend!

Packing for Alaskan fishing trip

Daydreaming on the plane...

DOGFISH
Northern
Lights
Return

Big Foot
is Seen...

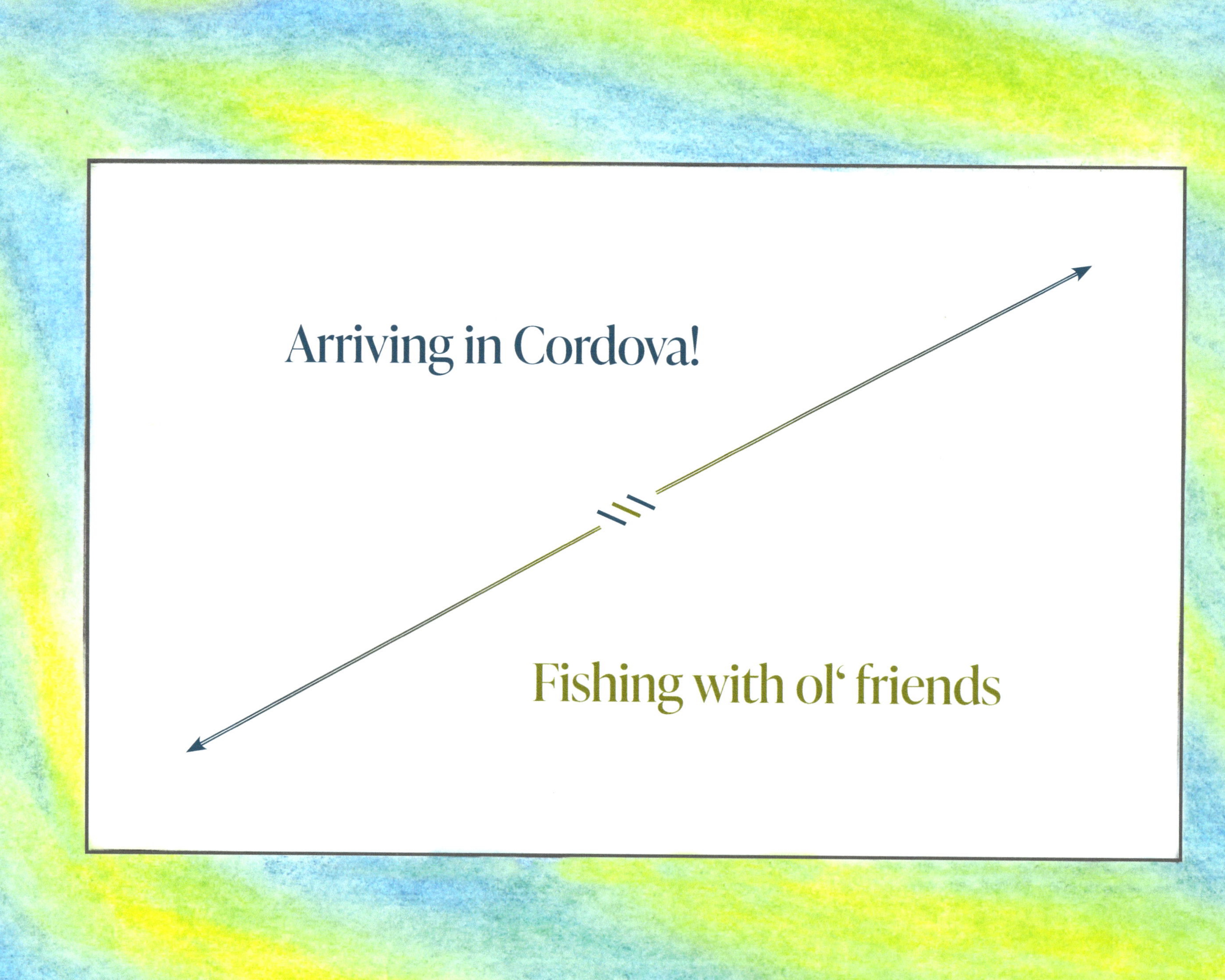
Arriving in Cordova!
Fishing with ol' friends

Welcome to Cordova
Alaska Air
ENTRANCE
BAGGAGE CLAIM
YETI

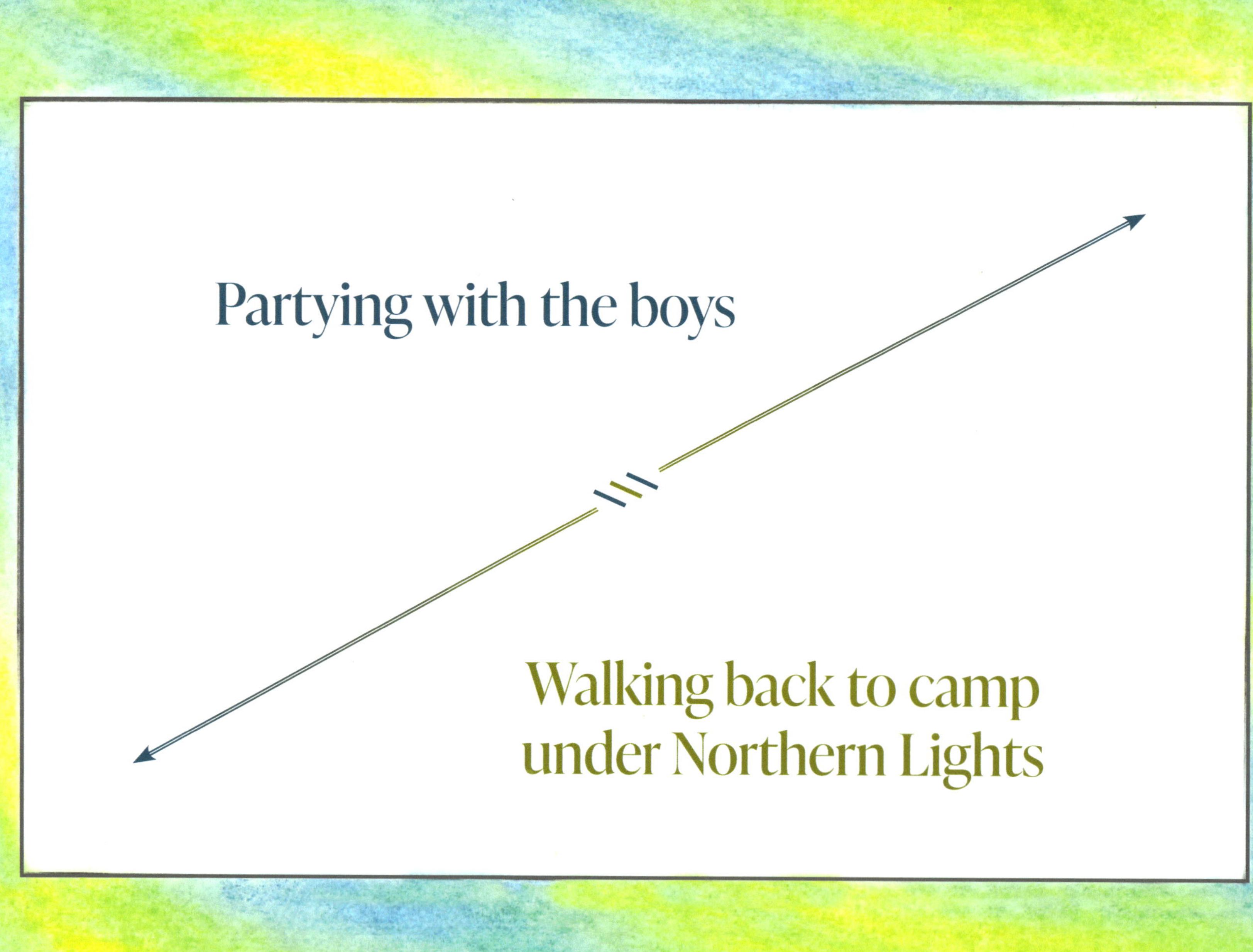
Partying with the boys
Walking back to camp
under Northern Lights

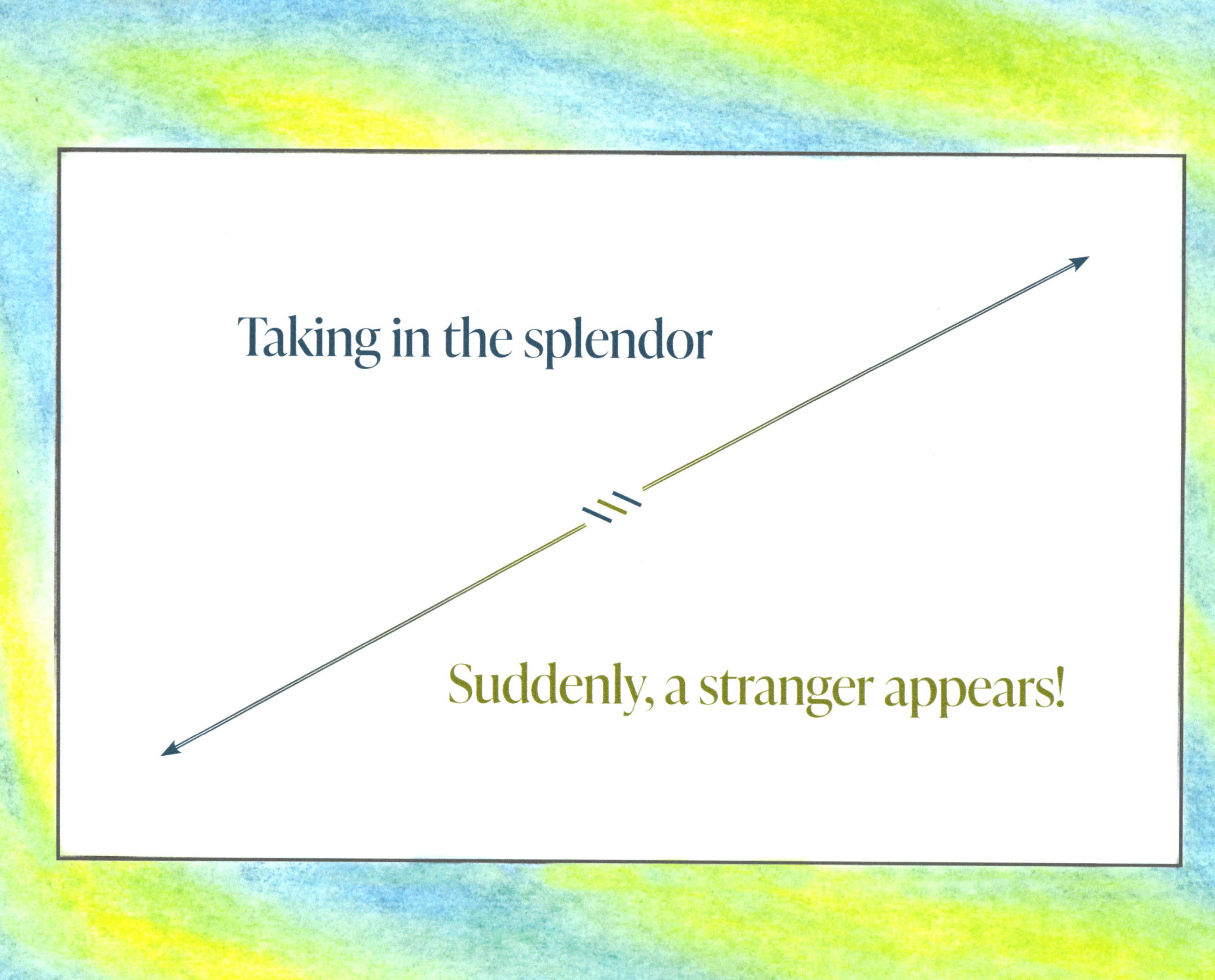

Taking in the splendor
Suddenly, a stranger appears!

Sharing a moment under
the Northern Lights!

OOOOooohhhaaaahhhhooowww!

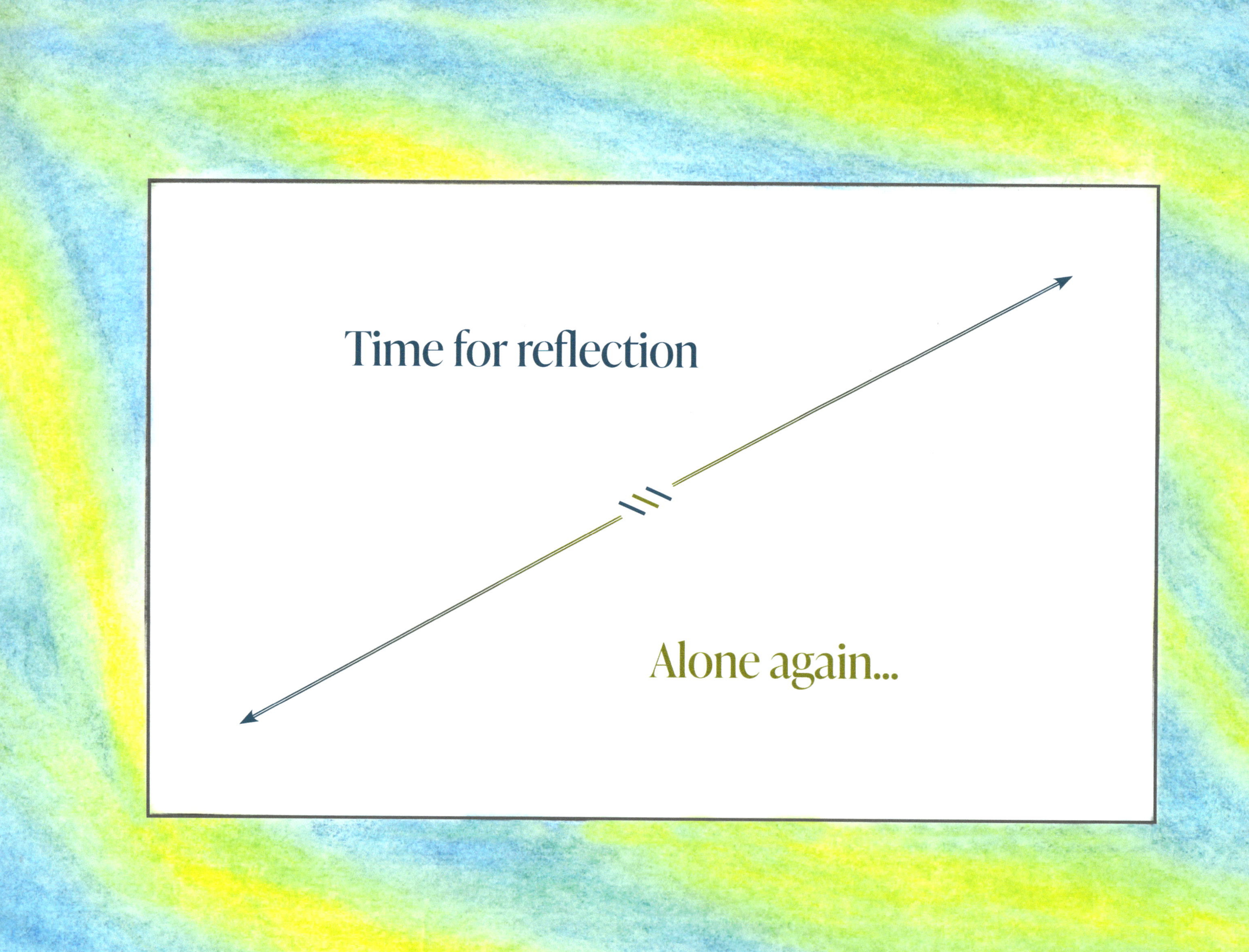
Time for reflection
Alone again...

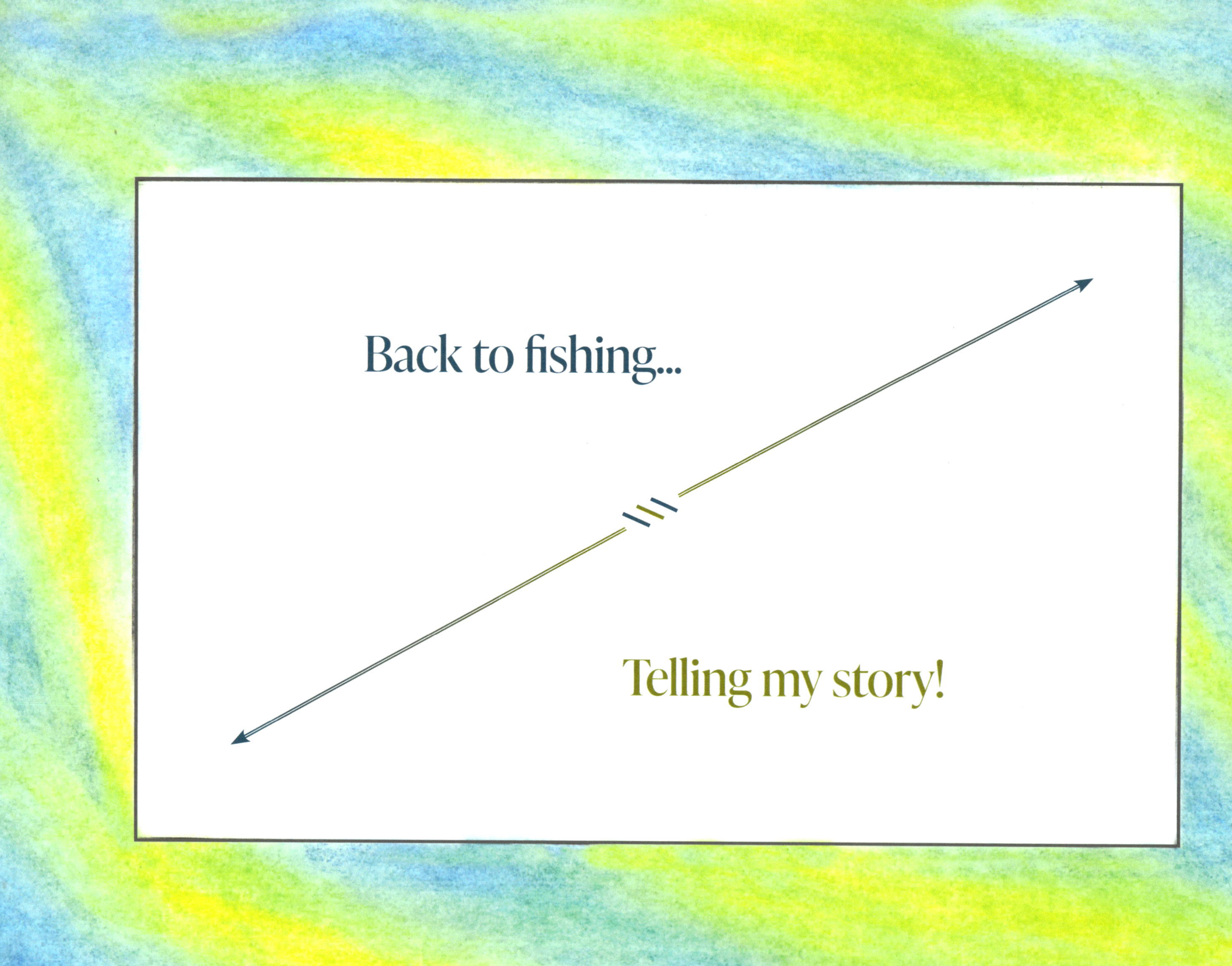

Back to fishing...
Telling my story!

Oooohha
Oooohh

Meanwhile, a plan is hatched!

A late-night visitor with a plan...

Gifts exchanged,
mission accomplished

1
ZZZZ
2
ZZZZ
ZZZZ
4
ZZZZ

One happy camper!

wiggle
wiggle
>click!<

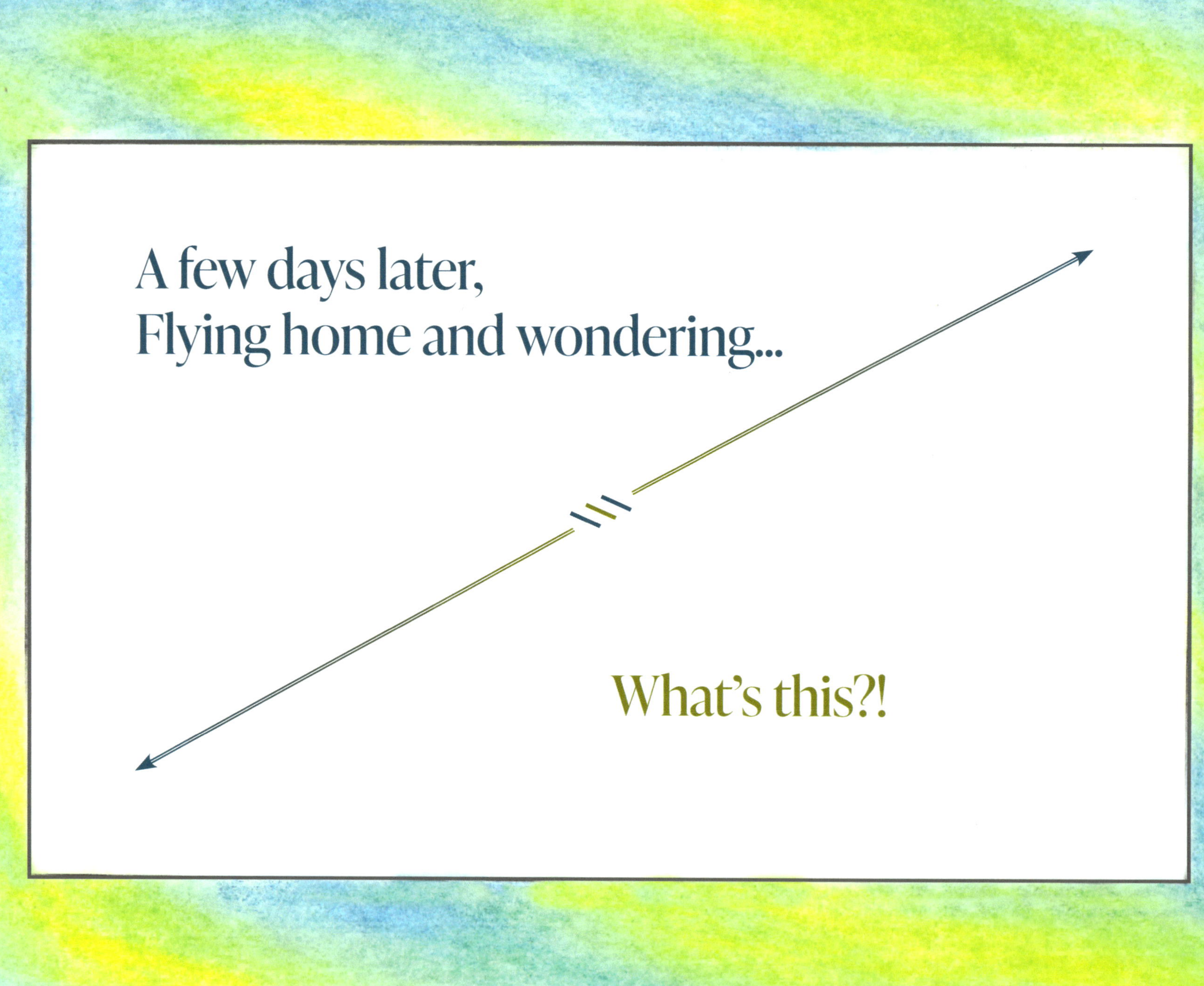

A few days later,
Flying home and wondering...
What's this?!

Forever connected

ooooohhawww
ooooohhawww
zzzz

Friends for life!

THE END?

Alden Sells is a song writer, musician and author who has been performing and recording in the Hudson Valley, NY area for many, many years. In the past few years, he has authored 3 books on how dogs affect us through out our lives. While Fishing In Alaska is his fourth book, where he takes on the role of illustrator. Alden continues to write, record and create...

And, oh yes - he still goes fishing in Alaska!

Nancy Stonecypher is a decorative artist who creates murals, designs fine art furniture and restores art work. She currently owns a brick and mortar store & art studio in Milton, NY.